Jason Takes Responsibility

Virginia Kroll

illustrated by **Nancy Cote**

ALBERT WHITMAN & COMPANY, MORTON GROVE, ILLINOIS

The Way I Act Books:

Forgiving a Friend • Jason Takes Responsibility

The Way I Feel Books:

When I Care about Others • When I Feel Angry

When I Feel Good about Myself • When I Feel Jealous

When I Feel Sad • When I Feel Scared • When I Miss You

Kroll, Virginia L.

Jason takes responsibility / written by Virginia Kroll ; illustrated by Nancy Cote.

p. cm. — (The way I act)

Summary: When Jason loses one of the invitations to his grandmother's birthday party, he is able to make it right at the last minute.

ISBN 0-8075-2537-5 (hardcover)

[1. Responsibility—Fiction. 2. Behavior—Fiction. 3. Grandmothers—Fiction. 4. Birthdays—Fiction. 5. Conduct of life—Fiction.]

I. Cote, Nancy, ill. II. Title. III. Series.

PZ7.K9227Jas 2005   [E] — dc22   2005003866

Printed in the United States of America.

10 9 8 7 6 5 4 3 2 1

The design is by Carol Gildar.

For more information about Albert Whitman & Company, please visit our web site at www.albertwhitman.com.

Mama said, "Who's responsible enough to do an important job for me?"

"Me," said Jason before Sam or Tyler could answer.

"Take these invitations to the mailbox right away," said Mama. "They're for Grandma's birthday party, and they have to be picked up today."

Jason took the invitations and started
down the street. Carson called from the park,
"Jason, come fly my new eagle kite."

"Can't," said Jason. "I'm doing an important errand."

"Aw, come on, I need some help," Carson begged.

"Well, okay." Jason set the envelopes on the grass
and ran to see the kite.

Jason and Carson flew the kite till Jason saw
the mail truck turn the corner. "Gotta go," he said,
running to get the envelopes.

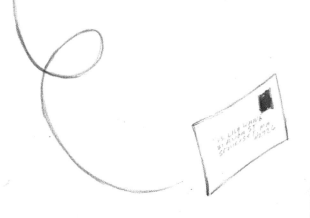

In his rush to meet the truck, Jason tripped on the curb. *Slide* went one white envelope, right down the drain grate! Jason could see it bobbing on the water.

Jason gasped. *Oh, no!* he thought. *Mama said they're important!* But now the invitation was gone, and there was no way to reach it.

"Oh, well, it's only one," Jason said.

He gave the rest to Postwoman Pam.

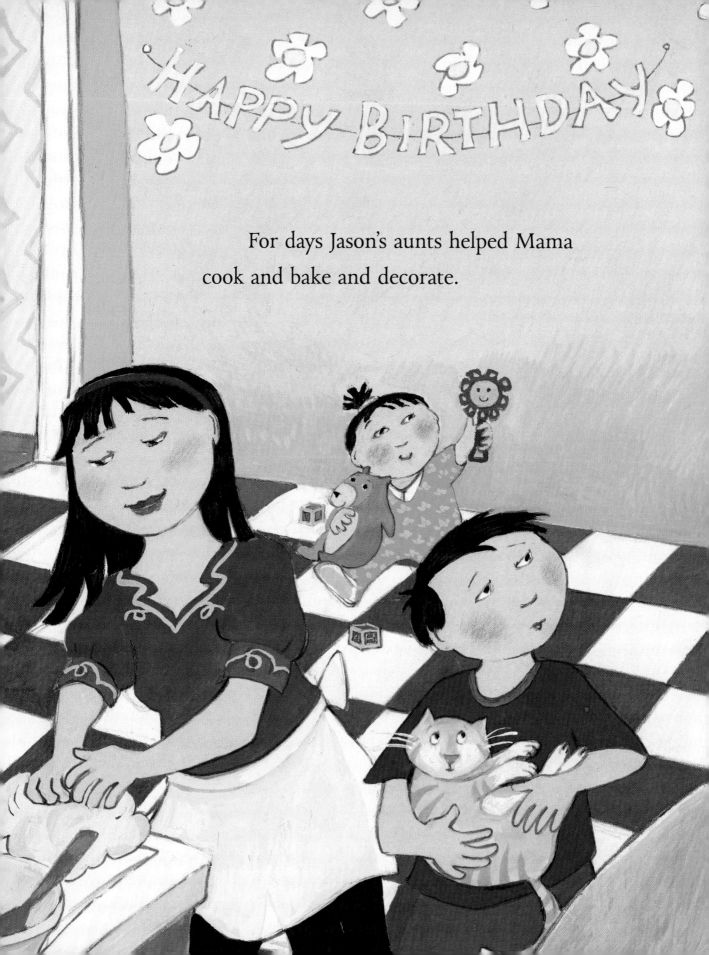

For days Jason's aunts helped Mama
cook and bake and decorate.

Jason thought he should tell Mama about the
lost invitation. But he didn't want to get into trouble.
Besides, he reminded himself, *it's only one.*

So he kept the secret to himself, and pretty soon,
he almost forgot all about it.

Grandma's birthday finally came. Everyone
hid, and then yelled, "Surprise!"

Sam said, "Grandma's so happy. Everybody's here."
"Almost everybody," said Tyler. "Grandma said
Mrs. Wang is missing, and she's disappointed because
Mrs. Wang is her best friend."

Mama frowned. "That is strange. I sent her an invitation, but I didn't even hear from her."

"Uh-oh." Jason gulped. "I think I know what happened."

Before Mama, Sam, or Tyler could even say, "What?" Jason was dashing down the sidewalk.

He found Mrs. Wang weeding her garden. He told her what happened. "I'm really sorry," he added, when he'd finished.

Mrs. Wang said, "I was feeling hurt that I wasn't invited. I'm glad you told me about it, Jason. I feel better now."

Jason finished weeding while Mrs. Wang went
in to change her clothes.

They came into the house just as Mama was
lighting the candles on the cake. When Grandma saw
Mrs. Wang, her smile was as bright as the flames.

Jason told Mama about the lost letter.
At first, she was very upset. Then she said, "Jason,
we all make mistakes. Next time . . ."

Jason didn't let her finish. "Next time, I'll do the right
thing immediately, Mama," he promised.

Mama smiled and said, "Well, I'm glad you decided to make
things right this time."

"Yes, Mama," said Jason. "After all, it was my responsibility."